RUBY THE ROUTEMASTER

RUBY'S STORY

London, one of the busiest cities in the world, is a place that never sleeps. Whether it is day or night the streets are always bustling. Many people live in the city, but even more travel in from the suburbs to work in this exciting place.

London is full of famous tourist attractions. People from all over the world come to the city to see the fantastic sights it has to offer. The streets are always very busy, and one of the easiest ways to get around London used to be the famous Routemaster Bus!

These big red buses, well loved by everyone that used them, transported people around the City for nearly fifty years.

This is the story of one particular red bus called **'Ruby'**.

Ruby lived in a London bus garage, and worked in the busy city centre, with her driver Dave and her conductor Clive. Every morning Dave arrived with Clive to collect Ruby, and off they would go to help the people of London get to their work, and the tourists, to arrive at the sights they wanted to see.

Ruby loved to drive through the streets, and to see the happy faces of her passengers as they hopped on and off her platform. Sometimes she was so busy, that all 72 seats were taken and many passengers had to stand. Clive, the conductor, walked busily, up and down her decks. He collected the fares and issued tickets to all the passengers.

At each stop Clive helped the passengers on and off Ruby, and then rang her bell to let Dave know it was safe to move off to the next stop.

At the end of a busy day, after dropping off their last passenger, Dave drove a very tired Ruby back to the garage for a well-earned rest. Ruby's favourite day was Friday, when Dave would take her to the wash bay for a nice warm shower. During the long week the dust and grime would collect all over Ruby's beautiful red paintwork, leaving her dull and dreary. After her wash, Ruby was shiny and fresh, ready for another hard week's work.

Everything in Ruby's life was wonderful, until one awful day. Dave and Clive arrived to collect Ruby for her day's work, but they were not their usual happy selves, they looked very sad. Ruby became worried when she saw their long faces. Dave told Ruby that the Bus Company had decided that all the Routemasters were too old to carry the people of London around anymore, and would be replaced with new, modern buses.

The drivers would now have to collect the fares, which meant there would be no need for conductors anymore! Ruby could not believe what she was hearing. What was going to happen to her and all her friends including Clive and Dave?

Later that day Ruby was parked in the station, waiting for her passengers, thinking about what would become of her, when one of her closest friends, Clarissa the coach, arrived.

Clarissa could see that Ruby was upset and asked her what was wrong. Ruby explained about the Bus Company replacing all the Routemasters with new modern buses, and how she would no longer be able to do the job she had enjoyed for so many years.

Clarissa said that she had seen one of these new, modern, buses at the depot, looking all shiny and very pleased with himself. She too was worried about what would happen to her best friend Ruby.

Several weeks later, Ruby returned to the depot after a busy day's work.  Dave was called into the office by the inspector.  After a while, Dave came out of the office, and stood in front of Ruby with a very sad face.  "I am really sorry Ruby, but I have some sad news.  The new buses are going to take our passengers around London now, and we won't be needed."  Ruby could not believe it, but it was true.

Very soon, Ruby was replaced, along with all the other Routemasters, by the modern buses.

Instead of spending her days taking all her passengers around the streets of London, Ruby sat in the dark at the back of the garage, feeling very lonely and unloved.  Her shiny red paint had become dull and faded, her tyres had gone flat, and birds were nesting in her engine.

Nobody came to give her a shower and make her feel good again.  She missed her friends and passengers a great deal.

One day, just when Ruby had almost given up hope of seeing anyone, ever again, she heard a voice calling her in the distance. She could not believe her eyes, it was her old friend and driver, Dave.

Dave explained that when they replaced the Routemasters with the new buses, all the Routemasters were sold to smaller bus companies all over the country. In some cases, they were sold to private collectors. Ruby had been sold to a bus company in Scotland, and he had come to take her to her new home. Ruby could not believe her luck. After a full service and a good clean, she was on her way to her new life in Scotland.

The journey from London was very long and, after several stops for fuel, she arrived in Liverpool for a well-earned rest. Dave parked Ruby in the car park and told her he would come back in the morning, after they had both had a good night's sleep. Ruby then switched off her headlamps, closed her eyes, and started to imagine what life would be like in Scotland.

Early next morning, Dave arrived. "Wake up Ruby," he said. "We have a long way to go today." Ruby blinked her eyes and beeped her horn in excitement. Dave climbed into the cab and started Ruby's engine, and soon they were on their way.

Once they joined the motorway, Dave could see a large car transporter in his mirror, the lorry was gaining on them very quickly. The next minute there was a massive **BANG!** Dave was thrown forward inside Ruby's cab!

The car transporter had not slowed down, and had crashed straight into the back of Ruby! Dave was very shaken and staggered from the cab. "Are you okay?" Dave asked Ruby. She was not all right. The transporter had caused a great deal of damage to Ruby's rear end.

Dave went to see the driver of the car transporter to ask what had happened. "I am so sorry", said the driver. "I have been driving a long time and I must have dozed off!"

The damage to Ruby was very bad and she could not move. Dave called the Police who organised a recovery truck. When it arrived, Ruby was hooked up, and taken off to a garage. Ruby was very sad, and very sore. She had been looking forward to her new job in Scotland.

What would become of her now?

The next day, an expert bus mechanic came to examine Ruby to see how bad the damage was. It was not good news. The mechanic said that Ruby could not be repaired, and she would never work again! Ruby could not believe what she was hearing. The mechanic said that she would have to be towed away to a retirement yard, where she would spend the rest of her days.

With a sad heart, Dave her driver said goodbye to Ruby, left the garage and went back to London.

Ruby arrived at the retirement yard and was put next to an old coach. Ruby was very upset, and began to cry. The old coach comforted her. "Don't worry you will be okay. We are all looked after very well here." Ruby was not convinced. She settled down for the night and rested her aching body.

One day, after Ruby had been at the retirement yard for sometime, a man and woman arrived. The yard owner met them and started walking towards Ruby. The owner said, "Good Morning Ruby. These people have come to see if they can repair you."

Ruby waited nervously as the man looked over her damaged body.

The man then said to the yard owner, "I think the damage is not as bad as it looks. I am sure I can repair her." 'Does this mean I might be able to work again?' thought Ruby.

"Ruby, my name is Chris and this is my wife Kim. You are coming to live with us in Somerset!" Ruby was so excited; she had thought she would be stuck in the retirement yard forever.

The next day a recovery truck arrived to collect Ruby and take her on the long trip to Somerset. By the end of the day, Ruby had arrived at Chris' workshop. The recovery truck gently pushed Ruby inside the building. "Don't worry Ruby," said Chris. "We will soon have you looking, and feeling, good again."

Chris started to remove the broken parts and her damaged body panels, in readiness for new ones. Ruby was beginning to feel better already, and could not wait to be back on the road again.

After around six months of hard work, Ruby was completely rebuilt. Chris arrived one morning and said to Ruby, "Today is the day that you will be repainted and have a shiny new coat of bright red paint." Chris drove Ruby into the garage and switched off her engine.

"Are you ready Ruby?" He asked. "Ding Ding", said Ruby. Chris then started to spray Ruby with her new coat of paint. Hours later, after a complete respray Chris drove Ruby out of the workshop. Kim was outside waiting for them.

"Oh Ruby, you look absolutely beautiful," said Kim. "No one would ever know that you had such a bad accident, you look brand new!" Ruby felt fantastic. She was lovely and shiny, and so happy to be back to her old self. She was very proud of her new look.

Chris knew there was no better bus than Ruby and that there would be lots of work they could do. With a big smile on his face, he told Ruby that she was going to be a very special bus, and they would have lots of adventures together.

Chris pumped up Ruby's tyres, checked her oil, filled her with fuel, and they set off for their first drive. Ruby proudly drove through the country lanes, taking in the beautiful countryside. As they passed through the town, all the people waved. "Ding Ding" said Ruby as she drove by.

Ruby was so happy. She was going to work again, this time in the countryside, maybe she would carry passengers again!

After a while they arrived back at the yard.  Kim was waiting for them beside the big barn that stood next to their home.  Kim opened the large wooden doors and Chris carefully reversed Ruby inside the big barn.  "There you go Ruby," said Chris.  "This is your new home."

Ruby could not believe how lucky she was.

Chris explained to Ruby that she would soon be taking passengers again, and instead of following the same route every day, she would now have the very important job of taking her passengers on special trips, to wonderful places.

Ruby was so excited about her new life, and spent her first night in her new home dreaming about all the wonderful adventures she, Chris and Kim were going to have together.